WELCOME TO
PASSPORT TO READING
A beginning reader's ticket to a brand-new world!

Every book in this program is designed to build read-along and read-alone skills, level by level, through engaging and enriching stories. As the reader turns each page, he or she will become more confident with new vocabulary, sight words, and comprehension.

These PASSPORT TO READING levels will help you choose the perfect book for every reader.

READING TOGETHER
Read short words in simple sentence structures together to begin a reader's journey.

READING OUT LOUD
Encourage developing readers to sound out words in more complex stories with simple vocabulary.

READING INDEPENDENTLY
Newly independent readers gain confidence reading more complex sentences with higher word counts.

READY TO READ MORE
Readers prepare for chapter books with fewer illustrations and longer paragraphs.

This book features sight words from the educator-supported Dolch Sight Words List. This encourages the reader to recognize commonly used vocabulary words, increasing reading speed and fluency.

For more information, please visit passporttoreadingbooks.com.

Enjoy the journey!

Little, Brown and Company

Hachette Book Group
1290 Avenue of the Americas, New York, NY 10104
Visit us at lb-kids.com

Little, Brown and Company is a division of Hachette Book Group, Inc.
The Little, Brown name and logo are trademarks of Hachette Book Group, Inc.

The publisher is not responsible for websites (or their content) that are not owned by the publisher.

First Edition: January 2015

Hardcover ISBN 978-0-316-40064-0
Trade Paperback ISBN 978-0-316-40063-3

Library of Congress Control Number: 2014943178

10 9 8 7 6 5 4 3 2

APS

Printed in China

Passport to Reading titles are leveled by independent reviewers applying the standards developed by Irene Fountas and Gay Su Pinnell in *Matching Books to Readers: Using Leveled Books in Guided Reading*, Heinemann, 1999.

MEET THE DINOTRUX

CHRIS GALL

LITTLE, BROWN AND COMPANY
NEW YORK   BOSTON

Guide to the Dinotrux

Cementosaurus

seh • men • toh • SOR • us

Craneosaurus

cray • nee • oh • SOR • us

Digasaurus

dig • uh • SOR • us

Dozeratops

doh • ZAIR • uh • tops

Dumploducus

dump • luh • DUH • kus

Garbageadon

gar • BAJ • uh • don

Septisaurus

sep • ti • SOR • us

Semisaurus

sem • ee • SOR • us

Tyrannosaurus Trux

ty • RAN • oh • sor • us • TRUKS

Velocitractor

vel • AH • sih • trak • tor

Millions of years ago,
Dinotrux ruled the earth.
They were like dinosaurs.
They were like trucks.
They were all very different.

Dozeratops had a big head.

He liked to push rocks and trees.

He wanted to meet new friends.

But the other Dinotrux were far away.

They were on the other side of the river.

"I cannot get there," Dozeratops said.

"I cannot swim."

Cementosaurus rumbled up.

He could pour cement from his tail.

"I would like to meet new friends, too,"

he said.

"We will need to cross the river,"

said Cementosaurus.

"I will put out a call for help."

He honked his horn.

11

Tyrannosaurus Trux heard the honk.

He was the boss of the jungle.

He did not like to work.

"I will bring my friends to the river," he said.

"We will build a bridge together."

Garbageadon came quickly.
"Maybe there will be snacks
at the river," he said.
He was always hungry.

Digasaurus had a big mouth
to scoop up dirt.
"We will eat after the bridge
is done," said Digasaurus.

Velocitractor had large wheels.

He could pull heavy things.

Septisaurus liked to drink.

"I am glad we are going

to a river," he said.

Dozeratops and his friends arrived
at the river.
"How will we build a bridge?"
Dozeratops asked.

"We should use our skills
to build the bridge,"
said Tyrannosaurus Trux.

Semisaurus carried things
inside his stomach.
"Inside my stomach are the supplies
we need," he said.

Craneosaurus had a long tongue
that could lift big things.
"I caught a tasty bug for you,"
said Craneosaurus.

"I do not like bugs," said Dumploducus.

"Please help me load these logs

onto my back."

Cementosaurus was very excited.

"Here comes the cement!" he cried.

He started to have an accident.

"Not yet!" shouted Digasaurus.

"It is not time for cement."

25

Tyrannosaurus Trux gave the orders.

Dozeratops moved the rocks.

Dumploducus carried the rocks away.

Digasaurus dug into the earth.

Septisaurus drained the water.

Velocitractor dragged the logs.

Craneosaurus lifted the logs into place.
Cementosaurus poured the cement.

The bridge was finished.

Everyone cheered.

All the Dinotrux said hello.

It was a very good meeting.

Then they all had lunch together.

And Garbageadon ate the most.